GL

KAH-LAN

KAH-LAN

The Adventurous Sea Otter

KAREN AUTIO

Illustrated by Sheena Lott

LIBRARY AND ARCHIVES CANADA CATALOGUING IN PUBLICATION
Autio, Karen, 1958–, author
    Kah-Lan the adventurous sea otter / Karen Autio ; illustrations by
Sheena Lott.
Issued in print and electronic formats.
ISBN 978-1-55039-244-9 (paperback).–ISBN 978-1-55039-245-6 (pdf)

1. Sea otter—Juvenile fiction. I. Lott, Sheena, 1950-, illustrator
II. Title.

PS8601.U85K33 2015   jC813.6   C2015-905349-8   C2015-905350-1

Sono Nis Press most gratefully acknowledges support for our publishing
program provided by the Government of Canada through the Canada
Book Fund and the Canada Council for the Arts, and by the Province of
British Columbia through the British Columbia Arts Council and the
Book Publishing Tax Credit, Ministry of Provincial Revenue.

Edited by Laura Peetoom
Copy edited by Dawn Loewen
Proofread by Audrey McClellan
Cover and interior design by Frances Hunter
Cover and interior illustrations by Sheena Lott

Published by
SONO NIS PRESS
Box 160
Winlaw, BC V0G 2J0
1-800-370-5228

Distributed in the U.S. by
Orca Book Publishers
Box 468
Custer, WA 98240-0468
1-800-210-5277

books@sononis.com
www.sononis.com

Canada

Canada Council   Conseil des Arts
for the Arts   du Canada

Printed and bound in Canada by Houghton Boston Printing.
Printed on acid-free paper that is forest friendly (100% post-consumer
recycled paper) and has been processed chlorine free.

To the hard-working people who protect or rescue sea otters, and to those who educate us about these amazing animals—thank you

To writers who have a story that won't let them go—don't give up

S. D. G.

"What a wildly wonderful world, GOD!
You made it all, with Wisdom at your side,
made earth overflow with your
wonderful creations."

—PSALM 104:24 (THE MESSAGE)

Glossary

Dark	night
Dawn	day
drift-tree	uprooted tree floating in the ocean or washed ashore
Elder otter	adult sea otter
furless one	human
furless Elder	human adult
furless pup	human child
Grand otter	old adult sea otter
land-tree	tree
not-rock	old green glass 7UP bottle
raft	group of sea otters; usually males gather in a separate raft from females and their pups
sea-meat	edible sea creatures
sea-tree	large seaweed called kelp
underfur	thick fur closest to the sea otter's skin
white object	Styrofoam float for a fishing net

CHAPTER ONE

Splash! Kah-Lan kicks his webbed hind flippers and dives into the cold sea. Yamka chases his bubble trail.

Kah-Lan darts to the surface. He bursts out of the water, jumping over a floating sea-tree bulb. Its yellowish-green blades sparkle on the calm ocean. The young sea otter dives again.

When Kah-Lan's head pops above the water, Yamka tackles him. Her white teeth flash as she play-bites his face. Kah-Lan breaks free. He speed-weaves among the sea otter mothers and pups to the edge of their sea-tree forest. He's the oldest male in this raft. His mother chases him and hisses a warning to stay inside the forest—again.

Kah-Lan ignores her warning for a moment, staring out to sea. There he would be free to explore, without her hounding. He could hunt for big crabs! *Here she comes.* To escape his mother, he quickly turns and swims back into the sea-tree forest.

Yamka nips his tail. He paddles hard to get out of reach, watching her instead of looking where he's going.

Slam! Kah-Lan crashes into a dozing Grand otter. Her ancient eyes fly open. They are raven black against her silvery fur. She glares at him and growls.

Kah-Lan's mother whistles at him. She bunts him away from the Grand otter to follow Yamka and her mother. They're leaving the sea-tree forest. It's time for the Elder otters and older pups to head to their hunting waters between the sea-trees and the rocky islands that slow the waves. The females with tiny pups stay to hunt in the sea-tree forest. A mother carefully wraps a sea-tree blade around her little pup to keep him from floating away. Even though he lets out a high-pitched call, she dives for food.

As Kah-Lan swims off, his grumbling stomach reminds him how hungry he is. He and his mother dash to catch up with the hunting group—last, as usual. If only he could find a big crab this time. It would fill his belly. The last crab he'd caught was too small, and his mother made him let it go.

While he's paddling, shrill cries of seagulls echo from way across the bay. The birds are whirling off the sheer cliff on the far point. They screech over food they've found. Kah-Lan stops and stares. What sea-meat is at the point? Big crabs, maybe?

The cliff calls to him: *Come and feast.*

His belly rumbles. Before his mother whistles at him to keep up, he again swims after the other otters.

The first ones reach their hunting waters, look around for any threat, then dive. Kah-Lan kicks hard to reach that spot. He's about to plunge to the sea bottom in search of food when an Elder otter growls a warning. Kah-Lan forgot to check for enemies. From the open ocean, a tall black fin is quickly approaching. *It's Orca!*

More sea otters growl. Some squeal, then dive. Kah-Lan's mother bunts him hard, pushing him toward the sea-trees. Then she dives. He should follow her, but he's tired of obeying. At least, obeying right away. He figures he's got plenty of time to escape. Even when Yamka hisses at him and leaves, Kah-Lan stays put. He's fascinated by the fin that's growing larger as the whale speeds closer.

Orca races toward the remaining sea otters, faster than any of them can swim. Their only hope is to haul out on shore or hide in the sea-trees. The nearest shore is too steep for climbing out. Yet still, instead of fleeing, Kah-Lan stares as Orca approaches. The young sea otter has never been so close to a whale.

Orca reaches the sea otters at the outer edge of the group. It leaps high out of the water. The whale's shiny black-and-white body is going to fall on the otters only a drift-tree length from Kah-Lan. Fear squeezes his chest. He squeals as Orca smashes onto the otters as they dive to escape. The splash soaks his face and he is whipped backward by the force of Orca's wave.

An Elder otter floats near Orca. She's not trying to flee. Kah-Lan hisses a warning, but she doesn't move.

CHAPTER TWO

The Elder otter has been stunned by Orca's landing blow. The whale opens its massive jaws, scoops her up, and disappears below.

Kah-Lan's mother returns and screams at him. Finally, he dives. His heart is racing. They swim to the sea-tree forest. Maybe Orca won't follow them in there. Kah-Lan hides between the stems of the sea-trees until his air is low, then heads to the surface. There, his mother clutches him. He tries to wriggle free, but she holds on tightly. Yamka's being gripped by her mother, too.

The sea otters glance around, clustered together. At a puff of wind, they all dive. When Kah-Lan's head is back above water again, his gaze flits between the far point and the rocky islands where the sun is setting. There, in the open ocean, Orca spouts. A mist of water and air shoots up high as the whale swims away.

When Dark comes, the sea otters' home bay is quiet once again. The Elder otters decide it's safe to return to the hunting waters. Kah-Lan and the others feed, then clean their fur in peace. Later, back in the forest, Kah-Lan wraps a sea-tree blade around his body to anchor him as he rests.

As the sun rises, there's no sign of Orca. But the otters stay

in the sea-trees to search for sea-meat. Kah-Lan is so hungry, he's one of the first to scan around, suck a deep breath, close his ears and nostrils, and dive. He knows he must eat a lot, and often, to keep warm in the cold ocean.

He thrusts his flippers, and his body ripples like a wave. He follows the sea-tree stems far beneath the surface. A fish swims near him. He moves toward it, but it veers and darts past, too fast for him to catch. Food that's easier to catch waits below. Like crabs! And sea urchins!

Kah-Lan dives deeper in the silence. The water is darker and more blue-green the farther he goes. He heads to where the sea-trees are rooted in the ocean floor.

Anemones wave their tentacles and sea stars spread their rays. Kah-Lan glides past them and the clams burrowing in the sand.

It's too dark to see well, so Kah-Lan's paws and whiskers work together, searching the ocean floor. He snatches a spiny sea urchin and tucks it in the loose fold of skin under one of his forelegs where it can't prick his side. After more hunting, his paws finally feel a second urchin. He grabs for it, but so does another sea otter. They tug and tussle. Kah-Lan ends up with empty paws. *No! After all that work!*

He has room in his pouches for more sea-meat, but his air is running out. Pointing his nose upward, he kicks. Up he swims, past snails that cling to waving sea-tree blades and around a giant octopus. A school of silvery herring flashes by him.

Kah-Lan surfaces and gulps a breath of air. Floating on

his back, he pulls out the sea urchin. He carefully squeezes it so the spines don't hurt him. The purple shell splits at the bottom. Slipping his paw into the crack, he scrapes out the mushy flesh. He stuffs it in his mouth and chomps. *It tastes so good.* But one urchin barely touches his gnawing hunger. Kah-Lan tosses the empty shell away and rolls to rinse his fur.

Yamka surfaces next to him carrying a clam and a rock. She flips onto her back and bangs the thick-shelled clam against the rock on her chest. *Whack! Whack! Whack!* Kah-Lan's eyes are drawn to the cliff on the distant point. Each time Yamka whacks her clam, the cliff's call gets louder in his head. *Come! And! Feast!*

He stares at the cliff. He longs to swim there and hunt for crabs. This urge is growing stronger every Dawn. The Elder otters have warned of a dangerous current and crashing waves out there. Even though there are short times when the current is slack, the Elder otters will not go to the point. But Kah-Lan is a strong swimmer.

He turns to focus on the white drift-tree on the beach. Its roots spread out like octopus arms. That drift-tree sheltered the sea otters many Dawns ago when a wild storm forced them out of the water. Then Kah-Lan's gaze follows the familiar outline of the tall land-trees around their home bay.

Getting his fill of sea urchins takes many more dives than usual. Kah-Lan drinks a little sea water. While the urchins were good, he craves tasty crab. It's hard to find ones that aren't too small in these waters. Other sea otters in his raft eat different sea-meat, what their mothers taught them to eat. They have big enough prey here. But the supply of good-sized urchins and crabs is getting low. Kah-Lan, Yamka, their mothers, and all the other otters that depend on these sea-meats must either eat differently or find new hunting waters—and soon. But how can they leave with the youngest pups too small to travel?

Kah-Lan flinches, remembering the struggle over the sea urchin below. Competing for food will only get harder. What if he could find new hunting waters right now? If the hunting is good at the point, could the crab eaters stay in their home bay? He *has* to find a way to sneak past his mother's watchful eye.

Her eye is on him now. If Kah-Lan does not start cleaning his fur, she'll quickly remind him. So he rolls and gives his chest a quick scrub. Sticky bits of urchin innards cling to his long guard hairs. He combs out the bits with his claws. Then he somersaults. That washes off the scraps. Yamka is busy cleaning her fur, too. Twisting and bending, she tugs her loose coat. She pulls a section of back fur around for a wash.

Kah-Lan sees his mother's light-brown head, still only several sea-tree bulbs away. He fluffs his coat by blowing air into his short, dense underfur as she taught him. He even remembers to whisk the water into bubbles to rub into his underfur. Trapping air close to his skin will keep him warm. Only the tips of his guard hairs will get wet.

Come and feast.

The cliff is calling, and Kah-Lan shakes his head. Drops of water spray all around. He's sure he could easily swim as far as the cliff and back. But how can he go without his mother noticing? If she sees him leave, she'll drag him back as if he were a small pup. The call in his head will not go away. He *must* find a way to reach the cliff.

CHAPTER THREE

A sea otter hisses. Is it Kah-Lan's mother scolding him again? No—the hiss is from an Elder otter on the edge of the sea-tree forest. Kah-Lan's muscles tense. Is it another Orca? He scouts the open ocean beyond the rocky islands that protect the bay. He sees no whale or black fin or even spouting. Then a movement catches his eye and he glances up. A dark shape soars far above. It's Eagle—their sky enemy.

Kah-Lan is too heavy for Eagle to carry off. It's the tiny pups—the balls of yellowish-brown fur—who are in danger. Their mothers clutch them to their chests.

Every sea otter tracks Eagle as it spirals overhead. Then it plummets, aiming for a pup. Its mother squeals and dives, carrying her pup with her. The sea otters nearby also disappear underwater.

Kah-Lan and Yamka curve into the water like dolphins. The rest of the sea otters dive, too. They'll stay below as long as they can so Eagle will give up its hunt.

This is my chance to sneak away! Kah-Lan slows to let all the sea otters pass him. They go straight down, but he swims toward the cliff. He presses his paws to his sides and pumps the water with his hind flippers. He flies under the surface. Thinking about finding a big tasty crab spurs him on.

He slides his nose above water to breathe. *Oh, no*—Yamka is following him. He won't let her stop him. With all his might he pushes his flippers against the water. His back end swishes up and down. Faster and faster he goes. How far away is the cliff? Kah-Lan can't tell or slow down to look.

Ouch—Yamka nips his tail, wanting him to turn back. Instead, he swerves to get away from her and paddles harder, even though his flippers ache.

When Kah-Lan surfaces next, he's closer to the cliff. The drift-tree with octopus roots is far behind him, on the other side of the bay. Down he goes, forcing his body to keep swimming.

Yamka nips his tail again, but he doesn't mind. They've reached the cliff. He grunts with delight. The wind sprays water into his eyes. He doesn't have to swim as hard now. The current is pulling him around the cliff. It looks like a good place for crabs.

Yamka squeals in fright and climbs over him. She doesn't like the current and bunts him back toward home. Kah-Lan ignores her and dives for the sea bottom. Where are the crabs? His paws and whiskers don't sense any sea-meat. He finds no sea urchins, no clams, and not one sea star.

He's about to run out of air when he brushes something with his paw. A large shell. It feels like a crab! It scuttles away. He returns to the surface and grabs a breath.

The current sweeps him along. Kah-Lan is not used to travelling so quickly at the surface. Soon he's fully around

the point. There, wind-whipped waves are crashing against black rocks. Down he goes, ignoring the danger. All he can think about is finding another crab.

Success! This crab is so big it's a whole meal. He flies to the sunlight, holding the crab's back to his chest to keep its pincers from hurting him. He was right. The big crabs are so close, the crab eaters can stay in their sea-tree forest, thanks to him. Kah-Lan has found new hunting waters! His mother will be so proud.

He surfaces a distance from where Yamka is bobbing. When she spies his catch, she eagerly hurries to find her own.

The seagulls circle above as they screech and watch for scraps. First Kah-Lan removes the crab's pincers. A gull swoops in and snatches one. Then Kah-Lan snaps off one of the crab's legs and sucks out the meat. *Delicious!* As he attacks another leg, Yamka bobs up closer to the rocky shore. She begins devouring her crab.

When his belly is full, Kah-Lan is ready to return home. Yamka is still cracking and slurping. Then she disappears. It's not a simple roll-and-rinse—she's gone. He searches the waves. Yamka does not reappear. He paddles to where he last saw her.

Suddenly, Kah-Lan is sucked underwater. What's happening? He tumbles and twists. How deep is he? His lungs scream for air. Which way is up?

CHAPTER FOUR

Kah-Lan kicks against the undertow. He claws his way to the surface. Yamka is nearby. He gasps for breath.

This is not the protective calm of their home bay. The waves around them are massive. They're attacking the rocks on shore. Water shoots skyward. The waves force the young sea otters closer to the jagged rocks. Yamka and Kah-Lan struggle to swim back the way they came, but the strong current charges into them.

Kah-Lan's chest heaves as he pants for air, full of fear. It looks as if they'll be smashed against the rocks! *No! We can't give up.* Kah-Lan coos, urging Yamka to keep trying to avoid the rocky shore. He glances back toward their home waters and can't see their bay at all. Even the cliff looks small. The current the Elder otters warned about is sweeping them far along the coast. Now he understands why the sea otters don't hunt at the point. It's far too risky. But somehow he and Yamka must return to the cliff and swim around it so they can return to their home bay.

Now the ocean is pulling them out to sea, where Orca roams. Kah-Lan swallows a whine. He's growing so weak his flippers shake. Yamka's struggling, too. How can they ever beat this current?

He longs for sea-tree blades to wrap around them so they won't be dragged any farther out. Tethered safely, they could rest for a while and then try again to get closer to shore. Yamka whimpers. Kah-Lan links his paw around one of hers. Wherever they end up, they'll stay together.

The sea otters float on their backs, with their flippers out of the water to keep their bodies warmer. Yamka's eyes close. Kah-Lan grips her paw even tighter. They sail on down the coast.

The land-trees are tiny. Kah-Lan has never been this far from shore. The sea is calm now, but his insides churn. If Orca discovers them, they're sea-meat.

Then Kah-Lan catches a scent: fresh drift-tree. They paddle toward it and find many drift-trees. He's surprised to see so many jumbled together. Their scent is strong. They're still covered in bark, but they have no roots or branches. The drift-trees are like an island.

Perhaps this is where the otters can be out of reach of Orca. They can rest in safety, then head back home. Kah-Lan drags himself onto the drift-tree island. He coos to Yamka to climb up. She's worn out, too, but hesitates.

Then the drift-tree island moves, heading away from their home bay. Yamka will be left behind. Kah-Lan urgently coos. She quickly pulls herself aboard and collapses. Kah-Lan strains his eyes to find a land-tree, rock, or drift-tree on shore he recognizes. All is unfamiliar.

Then he sees it. Just ahead of the drift-trees is a gigantic

shiny creature. Kah-Lan stiffens. The creature is black like Orca, but it has a sea-star-orange top and is taller and longer than Orca. It stays swimming at the surface. His heart thumps wildly. Is it a different kind of whale?

Why didn't he hold back and watch for a while before climbing up here? If his mother were here, she'd scold him and then haul him to safety. He's too tired to flee. Yamka is not moving. Even Kah-Lan keeps silent, aware that he must be more careful. They have no choice but to stay. The strange creature bellows and lurches, startling Kah-Lan with every sound it makes.

CHAPTER FIVE

The creature roars. It makes more noise than waves crashing against rocks. It's loud enough to drown out the sea otters if they should squeal, but they do not. Kah-Lan studies the strange creature that's swimming slowly ahead of them. It doesn't seem to know he and Yamka are there.

Their drift-tree island follows the shiny creature past a rocky shore. They travel farther and farther away from home. Kah-Lan whimpers. Will they ever get back to their mothers?

Raindrops begin to fall as clouds press in. The brisk wind whips the rain into Kah-Lan's face. He shivers and snuggles closer to Yamka.

His stomach complains.

To stay alive, he knows they need to warm up, and to do that, they must eat. They have to leave the drift-tree island and hunt. He pokes Yamka. She growls but dives with him through water bare of sea-trees. They plummet toward the darkness below. How far down is the sea floor? The two swim deeper, farther than they've ever gone. Kah-Lan's nose and paws begin to ache from the cold as he descends.

Finally they reach the bottom. Kah-Lan quickly noses around the sea floor. He pats all over but finds no food. His whiskers brush against rocks and sand. Where is the

sea-meat? Air is running out. Then his whiskers sense a shell-creature moving. He snatches it and tucks it in his pouch. He also grabs a rock. Holding the rock tightly against his chest, he soars to the light to eat his catch.

Kah-Lan slams the oval clam shell against the rock now sitting on his chest. His rapid bashing soon breaks the shell. Yamka pops up with clams, too. This sea-meat isn't his favourite, but it's food. He's so hungry, he eats every bit. Using her teeth, Yamka scrapes the flesh from the shell she cracked.

Kah-Lan's stomach cries for more. A wave flows over his flippers. He drinks a bit of water, looks around, then dives again. He's almost out of air before he finds more sea-meat. Sea otters couldn't survive on the small amount of food in these waters.

As Kah-Lan and Yamka feed, more storm clouds gather. The ocean swells and pitches the animals about. Cold spray hits Kah-Lan in the face and he loses his rock. The wind howls. Waves crash on the shore. He and Yamka link paws to stay together. Rain pelts their bodies. They cover their eyes with their free paws. It's impossible to keep feeding or to swim toward home.

Yamka squeals as an extra-large wave washes over them. It sends them tumbling and somersaulting. If only they could find a sheltered cove with sea-trees for protection. Light is growing dim.

Waves surge, pushing them toward shore. Sharp rocks

loom ahead, but the only way to survive is to haul out on land. Both sea otters aim for the bit of sandy beach squeezed between the rocks.

Kah-Lan kicks his flippers with a spurt of energy. Will it be enough? He strains and pushes.

Finally, his paws touch sand. The next wave shoots him up onto the beach. As the wave flows back to the sea, it sucks him along. He clings to a boulder the way a sea-tree grabs the ocean floor. The wave rushes past him. He scrambles toward higher ground. His flippers slap the rocks.

A huge wave shoves Yamka onto the beach. She struggles to find her footing. Tripping over their flippers, both sea otters climb higher up on shore. They lurch across stones, driftwood, and sand.

Kah-Lan and Yamka collapse under a grey drift-tree, gasping and panting. At last they're out of the wind. The drift-tree protects them from the rain. All they can do is wait for the storm to end.

As Dark comes, Kah-Lan's stomach roars in hunger. But it's too stormy to return to the ocean. Eventually, he and Yamka doze off.

Much later, after the sun rises and the wind is only a whisper, Kah-Lan is awakened by a squeal. It sounds like a sea otter pup on the other side of the drift-tree. Kah-Lan raises himself on his paws and lifts his head. He stares into the eyes of a furless creature.

CHAPTER SIX

Kah-Lan startles and growls. He's never seen anything like it. The furless creature is bigger than an Elder otter and walks on its hind legs. It has only a little bit of fur, which is all on top of its head. Its ears are big but flat and round, not pointy and sticking out like a sea otter's. What *is* pointy is the creature's nose.

Loud screeches pour out of its wide-open mouth. The furless one is blocking the way to the ocean. Kah-Lan squeals in fear and holds up his paws, balancing on his flippers.

Yamka growls. The furless one waves its paws and hops closer, shrieking again. Then a taller furless one rushes over, making deep, stern noises.

The sea otters squeal, then bare their teeth. They will bite and crush the paws of these strange creatures if they come any closer. The sea otters frantically look for a way out of this trap, for a path to the water.

The tall creature picks up the shorter one and dashes backward, the way Kah-Lan's mother would yank him away from danger. The furless pup points its claws at the sea otters and struggles to reach them. Furless Elder hauls its pup farther from the shore, to the grass near the land-trees. The furless pup yelps but cannot get free of its elder's grip.

More of these strange creatures are running along the beach toward Yamka and Kah-Lan. The way to the ocean is clear now. The sea otters growl as they sprint for the water. Kah-Lan tries to hurry but he trips on rocks and sprawls in the sand. Up again, he clambers across the beach after Yamka.

The sea otters fling themselves into the surf. They streak through the water with every stroke of their flippers. They are safe from the furless ones now. The sea otters roll over and over to rinse the sand from their fur. Kah-Lan can't ignore his gnawing hunger any longer. They must eat before trying to swim to their home bay. He dives deep, with Yamka close behind.

They find no sea-trees. On the sandy bottom, though, their whiskers sense the tiny movements of buried clams. The sea otters start digging. It takes Kah-Lan three dive-and-digs to reach the clams. Now he loads his pouches with the sea-meat.

Before heading to the light, Kah-Lan reaches for a rock but can't find one. His almost-empty lungs feel as though they'll burst. *Where* is a rock? At last he feels something smooth and hard. He clutches it and swims upward.

As he floats on his back, water pours out of the hole at the narrow end of the hard object. It's nothing like any rock he has ever seen. It's as green, long, and round as a sea cucumber and has red and white markings on one side. As Kah-Lan turns it around and stares through it, he can see his paw on the other side. Strangely, his paw looks green. This is not a rock.

He's about to toss the not-rock away but stops. He needs something hard for cracking these tough clam shells. Maybe the not-rock will work. He bashes a clam against the widest part. The not-rock rolls. Kah-Lan catches it just before it slips off his chest. He anchors the not-rock firmly at the narrow end and whacks the clam again. *Craaack.*

Kah-Lan slurps the firm meat and throws away the shell. Bash, crack, slurp, chew, and repeat. When his pouches are empty, he scans the open ocean for Orca. There's no black fin, so he dives for more clams. The two sea otters eat until their bellies cannot fit another bite. Feeling warm and satisfied, they lick, comb, and rinse every part of their coats.

Without sea-trees to give some protection to Kah-Lan and Yamka, Orca could snatch them far too easily. They must keep moving. Will they ever see their mothers again? Kah-Lan whines as he raises his head high out of the water, but he can't spot the cliff that marks the far point of their home bay. Yet he heads back the way they came, with Yamka close behind.

CHAPTER SEVEN

Before long the sea otters reach a group of straight land-trees sticking out of the water. The land-trees have no branches or bark and they are speckled with barnacles. Way above the water, flat pieces of wood connect the dark land-trees to one another, creating a high island. Kah-Lan sniffs strange smells.

A furless pup springs to the edge of the high island. It points one paw at the sea otters and shrieks. Kah-Lan veers away from the straight land-trees. Other furless pups and their elders appear, all pointing down at the sea otters. Kah-Lan decides he and Yamka are safe in the water. So they keep paddling around to the other side of the branchless land-trees. The furless pups jump and screech, waving their paws, but they don't dive into the sea and follow.

Kah-Lan and Yamka keep an eye out for threats as they swim along the coast. Among the land-trees and rocks, huge wood and stone objects cling to the hills. Their glinting flat eyes stare out to sea. Kah-Lan's flippers pump faster.

After paddling for a long time, Kah-Lan feels his belly rumble. He and Yamka dive but find nothing to eat. Back at the surface, they keep swimming. How much farther until they're back with their own raft?

When they round a point, they meet a strong smell: fish. They follow the scent. It leads them to white objects bobbing on the sea. Thin strands link them together. *What are these?*

Curious, Kah-Lan grabs one of the objects. It's lighter than an empty clam shell and feels warm. When he rubs its smooth sides, it squeaks. Is it food? He chomps on the white object. It's so soft his teeth go through it and get stuck. He pulls hard. The object breaks apart. It's dry and tasteless. He rinses the pieces from his mouth and brushes them aside.

Where are the fish?

Splash! Yamka dives and Kah-Lan follows her. He finds a mass of thin strands like the vast spider's web he has seen on the white drift-tree at home. Here are the fish, stuck in the web. They're caught by their gills. He studies the web, trying to decide what to do.

Yamka snatches a fish and tugs, but she can't get it loose. Now it's time for air. She heads to the surface.

When Kah-Lan hungrily grabs a fish, one of his paws slips into the web and is caught. In a panic, he twists and pulls. With effort, he gets his paw unstuck and swims upward.

Yamka passes him on her way back down. Above water, he greedily fills his lungs and then dives again.

He sees Yamka just below him. Her paws are gripping the web, and she's clenching a fish in her teeth. The fish is too big to fit through the hole. She starts thrashing about in a cloud of bubbles. *What's wrong?*

Kah-Lan gets close and sees one of her flippers is stuck in the strands. She needs to breathe, but she can't rise to the surface. Yamka releases the fish. She rolls and tugs—but her flipper gets more tangled. *She needs help!*

CHAPTER EIGHT

Yamka pulls desperately at the strands, trying to free her flipper. In a panic, Kah-Lan attacks the strands with his teeth. They can't be harder to break than crabs' legs.

Snap. He splits one. Then he breaks another. She's not moving. Is it too late? Has she drowned? Kah-Lan furiously chews on another strand. He yanks and twists. It separates and Yamka is free!

She doesn't move. Kah-Lan nudges her. Nothing happens. He pokes her. Still nothing, so he bunts her hard. She wags her tail once to each side. Kah-Lan swims beneath her and pushes her upward. When their heads break out of the water, Yamka sputters and gasps.

Kah-Lan coos to Yamka and hooks his paw around one of hers. After a while her breathing returns to normal.

The sea otters stop trying to get fish from the web. They swim off in the direction of their home bay. Kah-Lan paddles slowly, weak from hunger. As Yamka struggles to follow, he whines encouragement to her. They stick close to shore so that if Orca shows up, they'll have time to haul out.

The sun slips away. Moonlight flickers on the black water. In a tiny bay, they dive and find a few mussels to eat. Floating on their backs, they link paws and rest. During Dark, they

hunt again. There's little to eat. The still-hungry sea otters feel tired, but they groom and blow air into their fur to keep themselves warm.

In the pale first light of Dawn they set out again. Kah-Lan's only thoughts are of food and home. They glide on.

Farther along the coast, rough waves crash onto a rocky island. To avoid being swept against the rocks, Kah-Lan and Yamka head out to sea. Swimming so far from shore, they nervously scout for Orca.

Kah-Lan's nose twitches. He catches a scent he hasn't smelled since they left their home bay: sea otters. Have they found their mothers? Wait. The scent is not quite right.

Yamka grunts. She has caught the scent, too. Together they plunge forward under the waves. When Kah-Lan surfaces for air, the scent is stronger. In the distance, he spots the sea otters. He and Yamka race toward them.

Black noses and eyes point their way. These adult male sea otters are much bigger than the females in Kah-Lan's raft. They have light brown head fur.

The Elder otters are eating crabs. They growl. Kah-Lan and Yamka aren't welcome, but their stomachs demand food. Circling the males, they head toward the scent of the nearby sea-tree forest. Perhaps they can fill their bellies there before the males return to their home forest. Kah-Lan can already taste the sea urchins living among the sea-trees.

But before he travels the length of a drift-tree, he stops.

Kah-Lan cannot resist the crabs. Taking the risk, he descends to the sea floor.

Back in the sunlight, he tears into his meal. The closest male sea otter glares at Kah-Lan and growls. On his back, Kah-Lan paddles away using his hind flippers while he keeps eating.

Kah-Lan sees spouting offshore. *It's Orca!* He hisses. Yamka lifts her head high out of the water in alarm. Both of them squeal a warning to the males. How soon will the whale discover them? The shore is far away, and the youngsters don't know how close the sea-trees are.

A tall black fin heads their way.

CHAPTER NINE

Elder otters sprint by. They aim for the sea-tree scent. Kah-Lan drops his half-eaten crab and bunts Yamka. They flee together.

But soon she is lagging. Kah-Lan is weakening, too. He feels as if he isn't even moving when more males pass him. Then a Grand otter swims by him. Is it only Yamka, Kah-Lan, and Orca, now?

At the surface, Kah-Lan hears a rush of water. Is it Orca's open jaws? He can't look back. That will slow him down. Kah-Lan's nearer to the shore, but it's still a way off. He snatches a breath and forces himself onward.

His body aches. His flippers quiver. Which is closer, sea-trees or shore? The sea-tree scent is stronger now, but the forest is not yet in sight.

Yamka pulls ahead of him with new-found strength. Kah-Lan pumps the water desperately.

Suddenly a long yellow object blocks his way. He swerves in terror.

Inside the yellow object is a furless Elder waving a straight branch with flipper-shaped ends. The creature holds a silvery object up to its eyes. A bright flash startles Kah-Lan. It's hard to see.

Kah-Lan dives. He stretches his flippers and kicks hard. Up ahead are the familiar swaying blades and stems under water. Is Orca right behind him? Kah-Lan surfaces to gasp a breath and rushes on toward the sea-trees.

Kah-Lan passes an ancient Grand otter. He's so old and weak, he's struggling to keep moving. Kah-Lan is almost at the sea-trees.

Splash! Orca breaches, almost on top of the Grand otter. The crest of Orca's wave carries Kah-Lan forward. He can't quit now.

Whoosh. Yamka darts into the sea-tree forest. He dives after her, weaving between the stems. They keep swimming hard, reaching well inside the forest.

As much as Kah-Lan wants to stay below and try to hide, his lungs demand that he surface. His head breaks out of the water beside Yamka. He sucks in air.

The furless one is flashing its light at Orca. The whale is swimming away! Orca didn't attack the sea otters after all. The Grand otter reaches the sea-tree forest at last, just as Orca leaps like a dolphin and dives. *Flash! Flash!* Then even the furless one paddles away.

The male sea otters bob up from below, checking for signs of Orca. Kah-Lan and Yamka tense, getting ready to dive again. When they finally see spouting far from shore, they float on their backs and catch their breath.

Staying out of the Elder otters' way, Kah-Lan and Yamka keep to the far edge of the males' territory. The youngsters

hunt until their bellies are full. If only Kah-Lan could find such good hunting waters for his own raft. After grooming, the young sea otters sleep.

But not long enough. They're awakened by growls.

CHAPTER TEN

Elder otters rush at Kah-Lan and Yamka, growling and hissing. Kah-Lan growls back.

The males keep charging, so Kah-Lan moves between them and Yamka. Clearly these Elder otters will no longer tolerate the youngsters. Kah-Lan gently bunts Yamka toward home and they swim off. With a few final hisses, the males retreat.

After Kah-Lan and Yamka travel a long way, the sun blazes at its peak overhead. They are weary and hungry, but there's no safe place to stop.

They swim between an island and shore, then round a point heaped with drift-trees. Their noses catch a slight sea-tree scent. Both sea otters speed up.

Soon they spot the sea-tree forest. There are no other sea otters in sight. Kah-Lan and Yamka rush forward and dive to the bottom. Sea urchins! Sea stars! Crabs! What a feast!

At the surface, the sea otters coo and slurp. They grunt and chew. Kah-Lan dives for more sea-meat. *What a perfect new home!*

Eating such a big meal, Kah-Lan feels content and sleepy. He and Yamka groom their fur and feel warm again. After resting, they forage for food once more, then sleep until Dawn.

Kah-Lan remembers their mothers and the other crab and urchin eaters. How they would love the abundance here! He and Yamka must find their raft and bring the crab eaters to these waters.

Kah-Lan dives to get a crab, the largest one he can find. He rips off its pincers and gobbles the meat from its legs. Then he tucks the shell in his pouch. With this to show them, at least some of the otters at home will want to follow him here and start a new raft.

Now he's ready to go. He bunts Yamka toward their home bay. Instead of leaving, she tackles him and play-bites his face. Kah-Lan again bunts her, then swims off. She refuses to follow him. He returns and nudges her. She ignores him, draping a sea-tree blade over herself to rest.

Kah-Lan will not leave her here. Who knows what would happen to her on her own? He nips her tail. Yamka snarls but reluctantly paddles in the direction of their home bay. When she slows and tries to turn back, he growls, forcing her to keep going. The harder she resists, the harder he works, forcing her to travel along the coast.

A rocky point lies ahead. The cliff on the point looks familiar. Could it be the one that called to Kah-Lan: *Come and feast*? His heart knocks hard against his chest as he remembers being sucked underwater. Can he and Yamka beat that powerful current to make it around the point?

The ocean begins to push against them. Yamka whimpers.

Kah-Lan swims alongside her. They must keep going. What if their mothers have no more food?

Then the scent of sea-trees hits Kah-Lan's nostrils. It must be from their home waters. He paddles faster, careful not to lose the crab shell.

A light breeze skims the surface. Waves wash over the rocks below the cliff. The ocean is quiet this Dawn, and the current is not as strong as before, yet it still bears down on them. Kah-Lan's flippers scream for rest, but he doesn't give up. He and Yamka force themselves onward, bucking the current. They must get to their raft.

At last, they reach the tip of the point. The smell of sea-trees propels them onward. Kah-Lan pumps the water as hard as he can.

He and Yamka round the cliff, and the current suddenly lets go of them. Ahead, sea-tree bulbs glint in the sunlight. Sleeping sea otters float among the bulbs and blades. Some carry tiny pups on their chests.

Rocky islands guard the bay. The tall land-trees on shore stand in a familiar outline. The drift-tree with octopus roots is whiter than ever. Home! Kah-Lan and Yamka grunt for joy.

Yamka squeals at the sight of her mother and flings herself toward her. Kah-Lan lifts his head farther out of the water to search for his mother. He plunges to hunt for her among the sea-trees. Back at the surface, he weaves about, frantic now to find her. A silvery head pops up in his path.

Kah-Lan veers to miss slamming into the Grand otter. Her ancient eyes follow him.

Finally, he spots his mother as she surfaces with an almost-too-small sea urchin. He squeals and she drops her catch. She wraps one of her paws around Kah-Lan. With her other paw, she gently pats him. She coos. He coos back. He doesn't struggle to get away.

But before long, Kah-Lan's mother releases him. His puphood is ending. He's not afraid. He's ready to take care of himself.

Yet first he and Yamka must get their mothers and the rest of the crab eaters to follow them around the point. They have to go now while the ocean is calm and the current is a bit slack. Kah-Lan pulls out the legless crab and shows it to his mother, the other Elder otters, and the Grand otters. Then he swims toward the cliff. He grunts, urging other otters to come along.

Yamka joins him, loudly grunting. A few Elder otters glance toward where she and Kah-Lan are leading. But none of the adults move.

CHAPTER ELEVEN

Kah-Lan and Yamka keep grunting and paddling away from the raft. They don't know what else to do to get the crab eaters to come with them. So they keep swimming and calling.

The first sea otter to follow the youngsters is not Kah-Lan's mother. Neither is it Yamka's mother. It's the ancient Grand otter. She points her silvery head in the direction of the cliff and swims off.

Now the youngsters' mothers join her. Other Grand otters and Elder otters begin paddling toward the cliff. A few mothers clutch their small pups and swim after them.

Kah-Lan and Yamka keep cooing as they approach the point. They stay a safe distance from the jagged rocky shore-line. Once the sea otters can get around the cliff, the current will help them along.

But they're not far enough yet, and the Grand otter with the silvery head slows. Other Elder otters struggle to swim.

Kah-Lan circles back to encourage them along. He bunts the Elder otters and they continue swimming, rounding the point. When Kah-Lan reaches the Grand otter, he gently nudges her forward. Her ancient eyes close, but he refuses to give up. He stays by her side to keep her moving.

Oh, no! Kah-Lan catches a glimpse of Orca's fin cutting through the open water.

Squeal! He roughly bunts Grand otter. He kicks his flippers and pushes her around the point. Orca speeds after them. Kah-Lan screams a warning to the others up ahead. Can they all reach the sea-tree forest in time to try to hide?

Orca gains on Grand otter and Kah-Lan. If he leaves the old otter now and Orca takes her, Kah-Lan can escape. But is there a way to save her, too?

Swimming hard, he recalls when he and Yamka were first here. They were feeding on crabs closer to the rocks. Then Yamka disappeared, sucked under.

Suddenly Kah-Lan has a plan. It's their only chance.

He shoves Grand otter straight toward the shore. She feebly resists, but he's much stronger, pushing her on. The wind is picking up. Ahead of them, waves crash and spray the huge rocks.

There's nowhere to haul out. But if Orca chases them, Kah-Lan's plan might work.

With pounding heart and aching flippers, he presses on. The huge black fin slices the water behind them.

A drift-tree length away from a jagged rock, Kah-Lan turns. He steers Grand otter alongside the shore. It's all he can do to keep her from smashing into the boulders. He glances back at Orca's tall fin. The whale is still chasing them.

Then, in an instant, the black fin disappears. Sucked below. Is the current powerful enough to pull Orca out to sea?

The two sea otters don't wait to find out. They battle their way toward the sea-trees. It takes every bit of Kah-

Lan's energy to keep Grand otter moving past the sharp rocks.

Orca surfaces farther out in the ocean. Kah-Lan shoves Grand otter forward. Can they beat Orca to the sea-trees? After a blast of air from its blowhole, Orca aims for the two of them.

Kah-Lan spots the rest of the sea otters swimming into their new sea-tree forest home.

Desperately, Kah-Lan bunts Grand otter forward. Orca fights the current, swimming closer and closer to them.

But Kah-Lan gives one more tremendous kick. He and Grand otter enter the sea-tree forest. They dive, trying to hide from Orca.

When Kah-Lan and Grand otter surface, he scans the ocean. There is spouting farther down the coast. Panting, Grand otter can now rest.

Yamka spots Kah-Lan and coos.

Kah-Lan can't see his mother. Did she make it there safely? He searches until he finds her. But now she treats him like any other sea otter. No pats. No coos. Mothering him is over. He's free to leave the females' raft and find other young males.

But not now. Something calls to him. It's not the cliff this time. It's his stomach.

Dive and feast.

He's happy to answer and dives deep.

Crabs!

About Sea Otters

Sea otters (*Enhydra lutris*) are marine mammals that live in the North Pacific Ocean, along the coasts of Japan, Russia, Canada, and the United States (Alaska and as far south as California). A few hundred years ago sea otters were plentiful. Then hunters discovered their fur, the thickest coat of all animals. By the early 1900s sea otters were nearly extinct, and governments stepped in to protect the few small, isolated groups that remained. In Alaska the sea otter population grew significantly over the following decades, and in the 1960s and 1970s some Alaskan sea otters were relocated to suitable coastal waters elsewhere in Alaska, as well as to British Columbia, Washington, and Oregon. Today there are approximately 110,000 sea otters in the world. In the United States, sea otters are listed as threatened, while in Canada they are listed as a species of Special Concern (a recent improvement over their earlier designations of Endangered, then Threatened).

These well-adapted animals spend their whole lives in the cold ocean near shore. Sea otters dive for food, eat, groom, play, float, mate, give birth, and sleep in the water, and haul out on land only when injured, ill, or in extreme danger. Their homes are in kelp (large seaweed) forests and bays, usually in rocky areas. A group of sea otters—called a raft—may link paws to stay together or wrap themselves with kelp to keep from drifting when they rest. Rafts of female sea otters and their pups stay together, while males form separate groups. A mother will usually have only one pup at a time, and she devotes from six months to a year to caring for and teaching her pup.

In order to keep warm in the ocean, sea otters must eat a huge amount of seafood, competing with people for certain kinds of shellfish. Often, sea otters stick to whatever their mothers ate: clams, sea urchins, abalone, mussels, chitons, snails, crabs, sea stars. While sea otters reduce the abundance of shellfish in a location, they do not eat all of the shellfish, leaving enough of the creatures to repopulate the area.

The kelp forests where sea otters live also provide homes for fish, hiding places for grey whale calves, spawning grounds for herring, and protection against shoreline erosion and even climate change. Kelp is also food for sea urchins. By feeding on the sea urchins that eat kelp, sea otters prevent sea urchins from destroying these important kelp forests.

Hunting for food means diving to the ocean floor and searching with their front paws and sensitive whiskers. Sea otters' hind feet have long webbed flippers to help them swim and dive. These animals are able to stay underwater four to five minutes before returning to the surface to breathe again, but most foraging dives last one minute or less. Sea otters carry their catch in a fold of loose skin under their forelegs. At the surface, they float on their backs to eat their prey, using their stomach as a table. When their powerful teeth aren't quite strong enough to break a hard shell, sea otters will hold a rock on their chest and bang the shell against it. Unlike other mammals, these amazing animals can drink small amounts of salt water to quench their thirst. The rest of their water comes in the food they eat and the humid ocean air they breathe.

Sea otters must spend a lot of time cleaning their light- to dark-brown coats and blowing air into their thick underfur. Long guard hairs keep the underfur dry, and the trapped air helps the animals stay warm. Sea otters grunt or coo when content or excited; whine when frustrated; and squeal, growl, whistle, or hiss when frightened or distressed.

Animals that eat sea otters include orcas, sharks, and (for pups only) bald eagles. Hunting by humans is banned, but sea otters can get tangled in fishing nets and drown, and pollution, disease, and parasites are serious threats. The greatest danger of all is an oil spill. Oil quickly soils a sea otter's coat, allowing cold water to reach the sea otter's skin. As the sea otter tries to clean its fur, it breathes and swallows the harmful oil. After an oil spill, a sea otter will not survive without help from marine mammal rescue experts.

It is illegal to approach, touch, or move sea otters. People should stay at least 100 metres away from sea otters. This is for the safety of the animals and the public. Sea otters have extremely sharp teeth and powerful jaws—designed to crack hard-shelled prey—and therefore their strong bite can crush a person's hand, easily breaking bones. As the number of sea otters grows and the animals spread farther along North America's west coast, interactions with humans will become more common. If you discover a sea otter in distress, contact the nearest marine mammal rescue agency.

Further information about sea otters can be found in the resources listed below.

Fisheries and Oceans Canada –
Aquatic Species at Risk –
Sea Otter
http://www.dfo-mpo.gc.ca/
species-especes/species-especes/
seaotter-loutredemer-eng.htm

U.S. Fish & Wildlife Service –
Marine Mammals Management,
Alaska Region
http://alaska.fws.gov/fisheries/
mmm/seaotters/otters.htm

West Coast Sea Otter Recovery
http://oceanlink.island.net/
seaotterstewardship/index.html

Vancouver Aquarium's Marine Mammal Rescue Centre
http://www.vanaqua.org/mmrr/

Monterey Bay Aquarium
http://www.
montereybayaquarium.org/
efc/otter.aspx

Seaotters.com
http://seaotters.com/

To view captive sea otters through live web cameras:

Vancouver Aquarium Sea Otter Cam
http://www.vanaqua.org/
ottercam/

Monterey Bay Aquarium Sea Otter Cam
http://www.
montereybayaquarium.org/
animals-and-experiences/
live-web-cams/sea-otter-cam

Author's Note

In writing *Kah-Lan*, I had to imagine how sea otters would function in the "what if" scenario I created—what they would do in order to survive. I remained true to the natural behaviour of sea otters, except for taking artistic licence with the following:

- While orcas do prey on sea otters in some locations in Alaska, orcas are not a real threat to sea otters in B.C.

- In reality, male sea otters might not growl at young sea otters approaching their raft.

- Sea otters might not haul out on a beach in a storm, but as the young sea otters in the story are exhausted, I chose this action for their survival.

- These animals are not known to prey on fish caught in a net, but because the sea otters in the story are desperate for food, I included this scenario.

Acknowledgements

First draft to published book in thirty years must be some kind of record! I wrote the first version of *Kah-Lan* as my final project at Regent College for a course called "Books, Children, and God: A Literary and Theological Study of Literature for Children." I have fond memories of parking my lawn chair next to the sea otters' enclosure at the Vancouver Aquarium to observe and learn about these fascinating creatures. Many thanks to Mary Ruth Wilkinson, who taught that course and gave me encouraging feedback on the story.

My incredible husband, Will, is my unwavering support; he, our daughter, Annaliis, and son, Stefan, have faithfully cheered *Kah-Lan* and me on as I've continued to revise the story and seek publication.

I'm grateful beyond measure to my writing colleagues, who helped my story gain strength and clarity with every critique of the manuscript: Fiona Bayrock, Patricia Fraser, Sharon Helberg, Eileen Holland, Loraine Kemp, and Mary Ann Thompson. I want to thank beta readers Margaret Hope and Jenny Watson for their useful feedback. Thanks, as well, to Sharon Foster for sharing *Kah-Lan* with her Grade 2 class at Shannon Lake Elementary, and to the students for listening and offering suggestions. My Blue Pencil Café session with Bruce Hale at the Surrey

International Writers' Conference was most helpful in pinning down the genre. For their spot-on editorial critiques, thanks so much to Elizabeth Lyon (beginning of the manuscript) and Gloria Kempton (entire manuscript).

Much of my research about sea otters was drawn from reading books and researching online, but I am most thankful to the following for providing details of the animals' behaviour and/or reviewing the manuscript for factual accuracy:

- Lindsaye Akhurst, Manager, Marine Mammal Rescue, Vancouver Aquarium Marine Mammal Rescue Centre

- Sheryl Barber, former Rehabilitation Consultant, Marine Mammal Rescue, Vancouver Aquarium Marine Mammal Rescue Centre

- Jeremy Fitz-Gibbon, former Animal Projects Manager, Vancouver Aquarium

- Adrienne Mason, author of *Otters; The World of Marine Mammals;* and *Oceans: Looking at Beaches and Coral Reefs, Tides and Currents, Sea Mammals and Fish, Seaweeds and Other Ocean Wonders*

- Linda Nichol, Marine Mammal Research Biologist, Fisheries and Oceans Canada

- Jane Watson, Biology Department, Vancouver Island University

Years ago, when I first saw Sheena Lott's gorgeous ocean-themed illustrations, I dared to imagine her artwork bringing Kah-Lan and his world to life. Sheena, having you illustrate this book is a dream come true. What a privilege to again work with my substantive editor Laura Peetoom and my copy editor Dawn Loewen—the exceptional editing skills you both offer are such a blessing. Thanks to Frances Hunter for the beautiful book layout and design. Diane Morriss is, hands-down, the most supportive publisher ever—thank you for the many ways you encourage me as an author. Your caring manner ensured the best quality at each step of this book's creation.